Famous Animal Fables

Edited by Carol Huey-Gatewood, M.A.Ed.

Publishing Credits

Rachelle Cracchiolo, M.S.Ed., *Publisher*
Conni Medina, M.A.Ed., *Editor in Chief*
Nika Fabienke, Ed.D., *Content Director*
Véronique Bos, *Creative Director*
Shaun N. Bernadou, *Art Director*
Carol Huey-Gatewood, M.A.Ed., *Editor*
Valerie Morales, *Associate Editor*
Kevin Pham, *Graphic Designer*

Image Credits

Illustrated by: front cover, p.1, pp.24–27 Monika Filipina, pp.4–7 Anna Gensler; pp.8–11 Axelle Vanhoof; pp.12–15 Corey Tabor; pp.16–19 Erica Salcedo; pp.20–23 Lee Cosgrove; pp.28–31 Steve Brown. Courtesy Luma Creative Limited. All rights reserved.

Library of Congress Cataloging-in-Publication Data

Names: Huey-Gatewood, Carol, editor.
Title: Famous animal fables / Carol Huey-Gatewood, editor.
Description: Huntington Beach, CA : Teacher Created Materials, [2020] | Audience: Ages 12 | Audience: Grades 4-6.
Identifiers: LCCN 2019026471 (print) | LCCN 2019026472 (ebook) | ISBN 9781644913215 (paperback) | ISBN 9781644913215 (ebook)
Subjects: LCSH: Fables. | CYAC: Fables.
Classification: LCC PZ8.2 .F345 2019 (print) | LCC PZ8.2 (ebook) | DDC 398.2 [E]--dc23
LC record available at https://lccn.loc.gov/2019026471
LC ebook record available at https://lccn.loc.gov/2019026472

5301 Oceanus Drive
Huntington Beach, CA 92649-1030
www.tcmpub.com

ISBN 978-1-6449-1321-5

Table of Contents

The Proud Peacock

At the dawn of time, all the animals in the world got together to decide who would rule over them. The animals of the land chose the lion. The animals of the sea chose the whale. The animals of the sky chose the swan.

In time, the swan king had a beautiful daughter with feathers even more bright and gleaming than his own. When she was young, the king granted her one wish. The swan princess wished that, one day, she could choose her own husband.

When she was old enough, the swan king gathered all the birds so that the swan princess could find a husband who was worthy of her.

Birds flew from far and wide to meet the swan princess. There were black swans and white swans, geese and ducks, eagles and owls. Soon, the lake was alive with the noisy chirps and twitters of sparrows and starlings, blackbirds and bluebirds, kingfishers and hummingbirds, parrots, macaws, lovebirds, and more!

"Now, my daughter, you may choose whom you wish to marry," said her father.

There were so many beautiful birds, it took the swan princess a whole day to meet them all. Many of the birds were handsome, but one bird caught her eye. It was a peacock with a long elegant neck, an amazing fan of emerald and cobalt blue feathers, and a delicate crown upon its head. She thought the two of them would surely make a fine match!

She went to the king and said, "I choose the peacock for my husband, Father." And the swan king made his announcement: "With so much beauty here, it was a difficult decision, but the princess has chosen the peacock for her husband."

All attention quickly went to the peacock. He proudly puffed up his chest, fanned out his feathers, stretched his long neck, and pointed his beak to the heavens. He began to perform a strange dance. He hopped from side to side, strutted around in a circle, and let out a long squawk. Then, he bent over to show off his splendid tail feathers, wiggling his bottom from side to side at the swan king and princess.

The flock gasped with shock, and some of the younger birds giggled. The proud peacock had gotten so carried away, he had made a complete fool of himself.

The swan king was unhappy to see such behavior. "Peacock!" he cried. "Your pride in winning the princess's heart has made you behave like a shameless show-off. I won't let my daughter marry someone who makes a fool of himself in public.

You will not be her prince!"
The peacock was so embarrassed, he flew away as quickly
as he could, in a flap and flurry of feathers. And that is
where the saying **pride comes before a fall** comes from!

The Greedy Fox

It was a cold harsh winter, and the animals of the forest were hungry—especially Fox, who hadn't eaten a scrap of food for days.

"It's okay for Bear," shivered Fox. "She gets to curl up for the winter in her cozy cave, with a full belly, dreaming of warmer days."

"And Squirrel can't complain!" he moaned. "He's been burying his secret fruit and nut supplies all over the place for months. But a fox? A fox like me has to hunt for food whatever the weather!"

Fox shook the fresh snow from his coat and slumped to the ground. His tummy ached with hunger, but he was so tired and weak that he soon fell asleep.

He woke later that morning to the sound of someone's footsteps crunching on snow.

He opened his eyes to see a woodcutter pushing a large package into the hollow of a nearby tree. The woodcutter seemed very pleased with his hiding place. He whistled happily to himself and went on his way. He didn't see Fox lying close by, covered in a thick layer of snow.

Fox sniffed the air, hopefully. *I must be dreaming!* he thought. *Is that chicken I smell? Is hunger making me imagine things?*

9

Fox used all his energy to walk over to the tree, and inside the hollow, he spied the package. One sniff told him that this was no dream. It really was filled with delicious food.

How can I get to it? thought Fox desperately. *I'll never fit inside such a long, thin space.*

But Fox was so terribly hungry, he knew he had to try. He pushed his head and shoulders as far into the hollow as he could, then tried to squeeze in his body. Much to his surprise, he had become so thin that he could fit inside quite easily.

Once inside the hollow, he quickly tore open the woodcutter's bag, and his eyes lit up at the feast before him.

There was enough food to feed a fox for many days. There were two roast chickens, a side of baked ham, a loaf of bread and several rolls, huge hunks of cheese, and three big rosy apples.

Fox couldn't believe his good fortune. Within minutes, he had gobbled up a whole chicken. It was delicious! However, as he hadn't eaten for so long, his tummy quickly felt full.

But I can't leave all this food here, thought Fox. *What if another animal finds it? Or what if the woodcutter takes it away again? What if I don't find any more food this winter?*

So, despite his bulging belly, Fox kept eating. He ate the second chicken, the baked ham, the loaf of bread, the hunks of cheese, and all three apples. By the time he had finished, Fox had more than satisfied his hunger, and his tummy felt like it would burst.

"I should get out of here," he sighed. "I don't want to get caught by that woodcutter with his ax."

Fox tried to squeeze out of the hollow. But this time, he wasn't quite so thin. In fact, his tummy was now so big and round, he couldn't get out at all. He was trapped inside the tree!

Luckily for him, while he had been eating all the food, the snow had fallen so heavily that the woodcutter couldn't find his way back to the tree.

Greedy Fox was forced to stay in the hollow for many days until he was thin enough to squeeze his way out again. As he leapt onto the snowy forest floor, he promised himself that he would never be so foolish and greedy again. 🌀

The Four
Harmonious Animals

One sizzling hot summer's day, an elephant was walking along the riverbank, looking for a spot to cool down. He came to a wonderful tree with a big patch of shade beneath it.

It was a very special tree. Its branches were long, its leaves were green and lush, and it had sweet, ripe fruit. Most pleased with himself, the elephant lay down to rest. He had just made himself comfortable when a monkey appeared by his side.

"Oo oo oo! Excuse me, Elephant, but can you see any fruits hanging from the lower branches of this tree?"

The elephant looked at the branches above him. "No, I can't," he said.

"Well, that's because I ate those fruits long before you ever lay down in its shade. I saw this tree first, and it belongs to me!" said the monkey.

The elephant slowly got to his feet. "I am sorry, friend. I didn't know this tree belonged to you. I was just enjoying its shade. I will move on."

But just as the elephant said this, a long-eared hare hopped by.

"What do you mean when you say this tree belongs to you, Monkey? I was nibbling at the leaves of this tree when it was just a tiny sapling. I think you'll find that this tree belongs to me!" said the hare.

Monkey looked at the hare and said, "We are sorry, friend. We didn't know this tree belonged to you. Elephant was just enjoying its cool shade, and I have been eating its delicious fruits. We will move on."

A flap of feathers from the top of the fruit tree caught the attention of all three animals. There sat a plump-looking partridge.

"What do you mean when you say that this tree belongs to you, Hare? This tree would not even exist if it weren't for me! I dropped the very seed that it grew from, so I knew this tree before any of you!"

The elephant, monkey, and hare all bowed deeply to the partridge. The hare said, "We are sorry, friend. We didn't know this tree belonged to you. Elephant was just enjoying its cool shade, Monkey has been eating its delicious fruits, and I like to nibble on its leaves. We will move on."

The partridge looked thoughtful. Then, she flew down to the ground. She asked the three animals to stay.

"We all like this tree so much. Why don't we share it?" suggested the partridge. "That way, we can all enjoy its cool shade, its sweet-smelling fruits, and its tender green leaves. And just wait until you smell its spring flowers!"

They agreed, and the four animals quickly became great friends. From that day on, they worked together, as a team, to enjoy their special tree.

The hare and the partridge worked in harmony to harvest the fruit on the ground and from the lower branches. The monkey climbed farther up the

The four animals quickly became great friends.

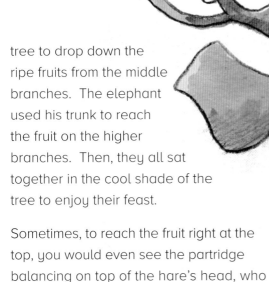

tree to drop down the ripe fruits from the middle branches. The elephant used his trunk to reach the fruit on the higher branches. Then, they all sat together in the cool shade of the tree to enjoy their feast.

Sometimes, to reach the fruit right at the top, you would even see the partridge balancing on top of the hare's head, who was on the shoulders of the monkey, who was riding on the back of the elephant!

Thanks to their friendship and willingness to cooperate with each other, the four animals never went hungry or suffered in the heat again. Around the forest, they became known as the four harmonious animals. ✺

The Crow and the Pitcher

It had been a long, hot summer. The sun had scorched the earth so that the rivers and streams had run dry. The animals longed for the rain to fall so that they could have something to drink.

A thirsty crow was circling the sky, looking for a puddle or a birdbath to sip from. It spotted a small table with a glass pitcher on it, hidden in the shady corner of a cottage garden. It flew down and landed on the table. When it peered down the long neck of the pitcher, the crow's beady eye saw that there was still some water at the bottom—enough for a drink.

At last! thought the crow.

Standing on the tips of its claws, the crow stuck its long beak down the neck of the pitcher and tried to reach the water. It was no good—the water was too low down. It tiptoed even higher and craned its neck as much as it could, but it still didn't work. The neck of the pitcher was far too narrow for the crow to take a sip.

I'll surely die of thirst if I don't drink this water, thought the crow. *But if I knock the pitcher over, it will all pour away.*

The crow hopped around the table and flapped around the garden, looking for something that might help. Then, it spotted a pebbly path and had a clever idea. It picked up some pebbles in its beak, then flew back to the table and dropped them into the pitcher, one by one.

With each pebble the crow dropped into the pitcher, the water level rose a tiny bit. The crow flew around the garden, grabbing more and more pebbles and dropping them in so that the water level rose higher and higher. At last, it was high enough for the crow to have a long, refreshing drink. Its life was saved!

Thanks to its clever thinking and determination, the crow was able to survive the drought that summer. He visited the garden every day. The lady who owned the cottage, however, never did figure out how her water pitcher kept getting filled to the brim with pebbles! 🌀

The Farmer's Horse

One wintry afternoon, a kind farmer was feeding and checking on all his animals.

He decided to take his favorite sheepdog's new puppy with him so that the little dog could get used to the farmyard. First, they checked on the sheep in the meadow. The frisky little pup barked with excitement when they greeted him with a chorus of **baaas.** He tried to herd them, just like he had seen his mother do.

Next, they checked on the chickens. The pup sniffed at them excitedly and wagged his tail, but he ran away whenever they pecked near his feet.

They also checked on the cows. When the cows gave loud **mooos**, the pup hid behind the farmer's legs.

Finally, they came to the stables where the farmer kept his favorite horse. She was a chestnut-brown mare with a long, glossy mane. She would often carry the farmer to town, clip-clopping along the road, proudly swishing her silky mane.

The farmer fed the mare well and always gave her the most attention of any of his animals.

When the mare saw the puppy, she wondered what this new little creature might be. The farmer patted the horse on the nose and greeted the stable boy, who was moving hay with his pitchfork.

The farmer sat down on a bale of hay. The little pup pranced and frisked around on his back legs, then ran circles around the farmer's feet.

The farmer and stable boy laughed when they saw the puppy so excited. They stroked behind his ears and patted his head.

The pup let out a high-pitched yap and jumped onto the farmer's lap, where the farmer rubbed his tummy.

So, this is how I get all the attention now! thought the farmer's horse. She broke loose from her stable, reared onto her hind legs, and began to dance about just as she had seen the puppy do.

The farmer and stable boy doubled over with laughter at the sight, which encouraged the mare to dance and prance even more. When the horse couldn't hold herself up any longer, she placed her hooves on the farmer's shoulders and tried to climb up onto his lap!

The little dog yelped. The stable boy rushed over with his pitchfork and shouted at the horse to get down. The horse was led into her stable again and put in a harness. She didn't get any treats or fuss that night. In fact, the farmer was quite afraid to ride her.

That day, the farmer's horse learned that it's better to win the affection and admiration of others by being yourself instead of trying to be like someone else. ⑤

Monkey Hats

There was once a hard-working young hatmaker who traveled from town to town selling his hats. Woolly hats in winter, caps in summer—he had a hat for every season.

One hot summer morning, he set off for market many miles away. After walking for a couple of hours, the young man decided to rest in a shady grove of banana trees. He put his heavy hat basket on the ground and settled down for a nap.

When he woke half an hour later, he saw that his basket had been toppled over and all of his hats were missing! He jumped to his feet and cried, "I've been robbed!"

There were no thieves in sight, but the hatmaker heard rustling in the branches above him. When he looked up, he saw a whole troop of monkeys, each wearing one of his brightly colored hats!

"Thieves!" he screamed. "Give me back my hats!"

But the monkeys just grinned and screamed back at him.

The hatmaker stomped his feet in frustration. The monkeys stomped their feet on the branches.

The hatmaker made funny faces. The monkeys made faces, too.

The hatmaker picked up a stone and threw it at the monkeys. The monkeys showered him with bananas in return.

Hot, bothered, and sticky, the hatmaker took off his hat and threw it to the ground. The monkeys took off their caps and threw them to the ground, too!

"Got you!" said the hatmaker as he gathered up his caps, stuffed them into his basket, and dashed away.

25

Over 50 years later, the hatmaker's grandson decided to take a rest in the same banana grove on his way to market. He, too, fell asleep by the trunk of a banana tree, and when he woke up, all of his hats were missing.

It wasn't long before he heard noises in the trees. When he looked up, he saw the monkeys grinning at him, all wearing his colorful hats.

"Aha!" said the grandson. "I remember this story from my grandfather...I know how this goes!"

He waved at the monkeys, and they waved back at him. He stomped on the ground, and they stomped their feet on the branches. Finally, he took off his own cap and threw it to the ground—but the monkeys did nothing.

The grandson was puzzled. "Huh? Why aren't you copying me, monkeys?" he shouted.

One of the monkeys climbed down and ran over to him. "You're not the only one with a grandfather who tells stories, you know!" said the monkey.

Then, the monkeys swung away through the trees, taking the hats with them.

The Lion and the Rabbit

The king of the jungle was a fierce lion who scared everyone with his loud roar and his huge appetite. He roamed the forest, eating any animal that he wanted.

None of the animals knew when the greedy lion might attack, and they grew tired of living in fear. They got together and came up with a plan. With knees quaking, they set off for the lion's den.

The brave zebra stepped forward. "Oh, mighty King of the Jungle," she said. "We have come to offer you a deal. If you can agree to eat just one animal

every day, then we promise that every morning, one of us will come to your den to be your dinner."

The lion thought this was a good plan. He liked the idea of lazing around all day instead of hunting. "Very well," he agreed. "But if I don't get my meal by noon, the deal is off, and I will hunt down every single one of you." To show he was serious, he roared very loudly.

The animals left the clearing feeling sad. None of them wanted to be the lion's dinner.

From that day on, they agreed to put their names into a hat every morning.

The animal whose name was drawn would go to the lion's den.

△△△△△△△

On the first morning, they all put their names into the hat, and the rabbit was chosen. The rabbit was the most timid creature of them all, but he was also the smartest.

He waved goodbye to his friends and hopped to the lion's den as slowly as he could, trying to come up with a clever plan on the way. By the time he reached the clearing, it was past noon.

"Why are you so late?" growled the lion. He was very hungry by now. "You broke the deal, and you're a pathetic, puny meal. I will have to eat your friends anyway."

"I'm sorry," said the rabbit. "It wasn't my fault. It was the other lion."

"What other lion?"

"Well, on the way here, I came upon another lion, and he began to chase me. I begged for my life and explained that I was going to be dinner for the King of the Jungle, but he wouldn't listen. He said that he was the King of the Jungle and kept on hunting me! I managed to escape, but I was very far away from your den and that's why it took me so long to get here."

As the rabbit told the story, the lion grew furious. "There is only one King of the Jungle!" he sneered. "Show me this other lion's den."

The rabbit bowed to the lion and led the way. He took the lion on a long and winding path through the trees to another clearing, where there stood a deep natural well.

"He was hiding in here, mighty King," said the rabbit.

The lion snarled and peered down the well. When he spotted his own reflection, baring its teeth at him, he let out a loud roar. The roar echoed right back at him.

"How dare you wear a crown! I am the King of the Jungle," he growled.

"I am the King of the Jungle," the echo growled back at him.

"No, I am the King of the Jungle," roared the lion.

"No, I am the King of the Jungle," echoed his enemy.

The lion became so angry he leapt into the bottomless well to fight his own reflection. The last thing the rabbit ever heard of him was a great, noisy splash!

The clever little rabbit hopped away, eager to tell his friends the good news.

Book Club Questions

1. How would the impact of the fables change if the animal characters were human?

2. How do these fictional animals compare with what you know about actual animals?

3. Compare the fables that include humans. What is the role of the humans in each story?

4. Contrast the "Four Harmonious Animals" with "The Lion and the Rabbit." How did the groups of animals work together differently to solve a problem?

5. In "The Farmer's Horse," why did the horse's dance get a different reaction than the puppy's dance?

6. "The Proud Peacock" and "The Greedy Fox" both include a consequence. Do pride and greed deserve such harsh consequences?